For the children of Mile 18

Printing History

1971   First Hardcover Printing, Tundra Books
1972   Book of the Year Award of the Canadian Association
            of Children's Librarians
        Runner-up for Amelia Frances Howard-Gibbon Medal
            as the Year's Best Illustrated Book, Canadian
            Association of Children's Librarians
        Look of Books Design Award, 1972
        One of the 100 Best Canadian Children's Books,
            Toronto Libraries
        A Choice Book of the Children's Book Centre, Toronto
1973   Second Handcover Printing
1975   First and Second Printing, Paperback
1976   U.K. Publication, The Bodley Head, London, England
        Third Hardcover Printing
        Third Paperback Printing
1977   German Publication, Jungbrunnen Verlag, Vienna
        Honor List, Austrian and German Kinderbuch
1981   Danish Edition, Carlsen if, Copenhagen
        Swedish Edition, Carlsen if, Stockholm
1984   Fourth Paperback Printing
1988   Fourth Hardcover Printing, Fifth Paperback Printing
1990   Fifth Hardcover Printing, Sixth Paperback Printing

Published in Canada by Tundra Books, Montreal, Quebec H3G 1R4
            in the United States by Tundra Books, Plattsburgh, NY 12901

ISBN 0-88776-015-5   Hardcover Edition
ISBN 0-88776-059-7   Paperback Edition

LC 74-179430

Canadian Cataloguing in Publication Data: Blades, Ann, 1947– . Mary of Mile 18. I. Title. PS8553.L33M3 C813'.5'4 C76-3598-9 PR9199.B43M3

Printed in Hong Kong by South China Printing Co.

Mary of Mile 18

Story and pictures by Ann Blades

Tundra Books
Montreal
Canada

Tundra Books
Plattsburgh, N.Y.
U.S.A.

It is a cold winter in northern British Columbia. At the Fehr farm snow has covered the ground since early November and it will not melt until May.

One clear night in February the temperature drops to forty degrees below zero and the northern lights flash across the sky. Mary Fehr gets out of bed and goes to the window to watch and listen. She hears a crackling sound and smiles, excited. Mary likes to pretend that if she hears the music of the lights, the next day will bring something special.

The next morning Mary Fehr wakes up happy. At first she can't think why. Then she remembers, and wonders what the day will bring. She pulls on her boots, hat, heavy coat and mitts, and walks to the henhouse to feed the chickens.

One winter day is so much like the next. What could happen? Her mother is expecting a new baby, but it is not supposed to arrive for another month.

Mary feeds the chickens and starts back. Seeing the house in front of her reminds her of another special day, the day her father finished building it. He was so proud. When the family first moved to the farm, they lived in the shack where the grain is now kept. Before that they lived in town, but Mary does not remember so far back.

Mary's mother has told her of the comforts of town: water taps, electricity, telephones and television. Here, water is brought into the house a pail at a time; the sink drains into another pail which is carried outside and emptied. The bathroom is an outhouse and the bathtub is a big bucket. The family has a transistor radio to listen to, but Mrs. Fehr gets lonely sometimes.

The closest neighbors are the Bergen and their farm is two miles away.

Mary sees her father near the barn. The caterpillar was damaged yesterday, and he is trying to fix it. Every winter day when it does not snow, Mr. Fehr likes to clear a little more land. He uses the cat to push the trees down and into piles.

When summer comes all the family will pick roots, tearing them out of the earth with their hands so that the land can be planted.

"When we clear most of this land, the Government will give us the deed to it," her father explained. "This is why we have moved north; so that we can have our own farm and live our own way."

Before he comes in for breakfast,
Mr. Fehr puts a propane torch
under the truck to warm the engine.
It will take an hour to warm
because last night was so cold.

Usually Mary likes this time just
before they set out for school.
Mr. Fehr is playing with little Eva.
Isaac and Jake are looking at
a book from the class library. This
morning Sarah tries to get Mary
to crayon with her, but Mary can't
keep her mind on it. What could
happen today? She is anxious to get
to school.

Mrs. Fehr serves breakfast. After the
new baby comes, the girls will
help even more than now. They will
do dishes, cook meals, make beds
and scrub floors. But they won't mind
A new baby is so exciting.

The radio is on. The weather report is
''Snow this afternoon. Clearing and
colder towards evening.''

Mr. Fehr goes out first and starts
the engine. He lets it run for a
while, then honks the horn. Mary,
Sarah, Jake and Isaac come out and
crowd into the seat beside him.
It is a tight squeeze, but it is also nice
and warm.

Today the teacher, Mrs. Burns,
has turned the oil heater on full, but
the room is still so cold that the
children sitting beside the windows
keep their coats on and edge closer
to the heater. At noontime Sarah
watches the class while Mrs. Burns
goes to the back to have her lunch.
At three o'clock Mary helps dress the
smaller children. She ties their
scarves over their heads and across
their faces to protect them from
the cold.

Mary sighs as she pulls on her own
overshoes. School is over for the day
and still nothing special has happene

In the truck on the way home,
Mr. Fehr listens to the children talk
about school but does not talk
himself. He is watching the road
carefully. Snow is drifting and it
is hard to see.

Just as they near their farm, another
truck looms out of the blowing
snow. Mr. Fehr steers quickly to the
right to avoid an accident and
his back wheels slide into the ditch.

As Mary watches her father jack up
the truck and put chains on the rear
tires, she thinks, ''I hope *that's*
not the special thing.''

Then, farther up the road to the
house, Mary sees something in the
snow and cries: ''Look, a puppy.''
She runs to him, kneels down, and
the puppy licks her mitt.

Mary carries the pup to the truck.
"Please, father, can I keep him?"

Mr. Fehr shakes his head. "You
know the rules. Our animals must
work for us or give us food."

Mary protests: "A dog can help . . . .

Mr. Fehr interrupts: "That isn't a
regular dog. He's part wolf,
and wolf-pups are useless. Take him
into the woods and leave him.
Come on the rest of you. Chores."

Sadly Mary goes off with the pup
while the others go about their jobs.
Jake goes to the woodpile, takes
an axe, splits logs and carries them,
an armful at a time, into the
house. Both the wood stove that
Mrs. Fehr uses for cooking and
the barrel heater that warms the hous
take a lot of wood. Sometimes even
when both are going, the house is
chilly.

The pup snuggles in Mary's arms
as she carries him into the woods.
How she wishes she could keep him!
"I would call you Wolf," she says.

It has stopped snowing, but the
path is covered over and the trees
seem to grow closer and closer
together. If she goes too far from
the road, she might not be able
to find her way back. She puts the
pup down to see what will happen.
He runs around, excited, sniffing
at the trees. She turns and walks
away. He does not follow.

"That was something special
alright," Mary thinks, as she walks
home, "but it didn't last for long."

Near the house Isaac passes her
on their horse, Mouse. A few years
ago Isaac and Jake rode Mouse
to school and kept her in the barn
behind the schoolhouse. But now
Mouse has to wait until Isaac gets
home to go for a run.

The house smells of fresh-baked
bread as Mary enters. Her mother
looks up from the stove.

''Where have you been, Mary?
Sarah is waiting for you. I'm almost
out of water.''

Silently Mary bends down, takes
two empty buckets standing near the
door and goes out.

Sarah has already filled her buckets with snow. Mary does the same and the two girls carry the snow into the house and dump it into a big barrel. They wait for it to melt, then go out for more snow.

From the barrel comes all the water for drinking, cooking and washing. Tomorrow Mrs. Fehr will wash clothes and Sarah will stay home to help, so the barrel must be full tonight. In spring and summer, it is much easier. A barrel catches rain water from the roof, and the river is unfrozen. But in winter all the water comes from snow. When the snow is dry and powdery like today, it takes many trips to fill the barrel.

Each time Mary goes out, she looks toward the woods. Her father comes out of the barn where he has been feeding the pigs and goes into the house. Isaac returns with Mouse. The pup is nowhere in sight.

The coal oil lamp is lit and Mary sits at the table staring at her reader. Mrs. Fehr is making supper. Mr. Fehr is cleaning his gun. The radio says another cold night, and Mary thinks about the pup.

Suddenly there is a sound outside the door, a low whimper. Mr. Fehr goes to the door and opens it. Mary cries: "It's little Wolf," and rushes to take the pup in her arms.

Mr. Fehr is angry. "Why are you encouraging him to stay around? Get your coat on and get rid of him so that he doesn't come back."

This time Mary walks nearly two miles to the Bergen farm. "Perhaps Mr. Bergen will let his children keep you," she says, putting Wolf down near the door. "Then I can see you sometimes."

As she runs home in the cold night her toes and fingertips sting and the air burns her throat.

The family is at the supper table when she gets back. Her mother looks up, says: "We have your favorite supper tonight, Mary. Moose steak."

"I don't want to eat, mother."

Mrs. Fehr starts to object, but Mr. Fehr stops her: "Let the girl go to bed without eating if she wants to." His voice is still angry. "She should not have asked to keep the animal. She knows the rules."

Mary gets into bed and buries her head in her pillow. "Why should he be so angry?" she wonders. Then she remembers last fall when Jake and Isaac begged their father for a gun of their own. He refused and got angry then, too. Her mother explained: "Your father gives you everything he can. When you ask for more, it hurts him to refuse. That is why he gets angry."

Mary lies thinking about this until she falls asleep.

That night when everyone in the
Fehr house is asleep, another
kind of animal, a coyote, comes out
of the woods. He sniffs at all
the buildings, then stops at the
henhouse. Silently he paws at
the rope that holds the door shut,
and the rope comes loose. The
coyote pushes the door to enter the
henhouse and get at the chickens.

Suddenly, a shrill screech goes up
in the night.

Everyone in the Fehr house wakes up
Mr. Fehr throws his clothes on
quickly, grabs his gun and goes out.

The rest of the family get up and
crowd around the window to see
what is happening. All except Mary.
She hears Isaac say, ''It's just
a coyote,'' and she tries to go back
to sleep, so that she won't have
to think about little Wolf out in
the woods.

Mr. Fehr sees the coyote in the
bright light from the snow. He aims
his gun and fires.

His first shot misses. The coyote turns, snarling, then quickly runs behind the henhouse. Mr. Fehr fires again, but the coyote takes off and disappears over the hill.

Mr. Fehr goes to the henhouse, looks inside to make sure the chicken are alright. Then he carefully ties the door tight. He is about to return t the house when he sees something at his feet.

It is the wolf-pup wagging his tail.

"So it was you who warned us,"
Mr. Fehr says. He bends down,
takes the puppy in his hands and
looks at him. "Tough little fellow,
aren't you? Not afraid of cold or
coyotes. Maybe you will earn your
keep after all."

He carries the pup into the house.
Mrs. Fehr has lit the oil lamp and
everyone is waiting for him, except
Mary.

The children get excited when they
see the wolf-pup. Mr. Fehr puts
his finger to his lips as a sign for
them to be silent. He goes to the
bedroom.

Mary looks up as her father comes into the bedroom. He puts the wolf-pup down on the bed. ''This little fellow would like to get warm,'' he says.

Mary can hardly believe she is not dreaming as she takes little Wolf in her arms. ''Can I keep him?'' she asks.

''I suppose you can,'' her father answers gruffly.

In the doorway of the bedroom, Isaac and Jake and Sarah and Mrs. Fehr, holding Eva in her arms, are all standing watching and smiling.

Mile 18 is a real place, even though it is too small to appear on the map of Canada. If you would like to visit it, you must travel north on the Alaska Highway for seventy-three miles, then turn right onto a gravel road. When you have driven eighteen miles along this road, you will come to the little Mennonite community of Mile 18 where the Fehrs and the Bergens live. If you would like some idea of where it is on the map, the closest town is Fort St. John, British Columbia, forty-five miles away.